Published 2008 by Concordia Publishing House, 3558 S. Jefferson Avenue, St. Louis, MO 63118-3968
1-800-325-3040 • www.cph.org

Text © 2008 Dandi Daley Mackall
Illustrations © 2008 by Concordia Publishing House

Manufactured in China

1 2 3 4 5 6 7 8 9 10   17 16 15 14 13 12 11 10 09 08

Thank You for Thanksgiving

Dandi Daley Mackall

John Walker, Illustrator

CONCORDIA PUBLISHING HOUSE · SAINT LOUIS

Pumpkin pie is in the air.
Sneak a taste? I wouldn't dare!
Set out fancy silverware.

Hurray! Today's Thanksgiving.

Making name cards—I know how.
I can smell the turkey—WOW!

Shouldn't Gramps be here by now,
Now that it's Thanksgiving?

In the kitchen, Mom is singing.
Here they come! The doorbell's ringing!

How much food is Grandma bringing?
Welcome to Thanksgiving!

Cousin Roger's at the door,
Looking **taller** than before.

Cousin Emma, many more.
Greetings on Thanksgiving!

Gramps and Grandma, come on in!
Uncle Earl and Auntie Vin,

Dinner's ready.
Let's begin!

Time to start Thanksgiving.

At the table,
find your places.
Look at all the
smiling faces!

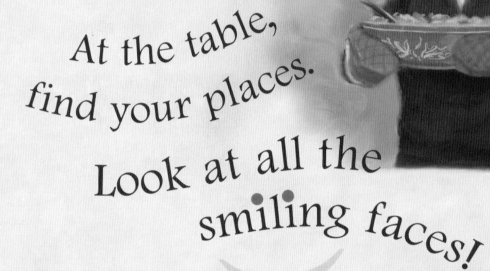

Let's give thanks for all God's graces.
Thanks for this Thanksgiving.

Gramps goes first,
which means I'm last:
"Thanks for loved ones from our past."

Guess I better think real fast ...

What am **I** thankful for?

Grandma prays when Gramps is done: "Thanks for loving everyone,

Sending us Your only Son... So much to be thankful for!"

Mom and Dad give thanks for **me**,
For all our friends and family.

What's **my** prayer supposed to be?
What am I thankful for?

Roger's thankful he can play
Sports like football every day.

That's what I was going to say!
Now what am I thankful for?

What's a kid like me to do?
Talk to God and say what's true.

"Lord, can I give thanks for **You**?
And thank **You** for Thanksgiving!"

And whatever you do, in word or deed,
do everything in the name of the Lord Jesus,
giving thanks to God the Father through Him.

Colossians 3:17

HOLY BIBLE